AF405943

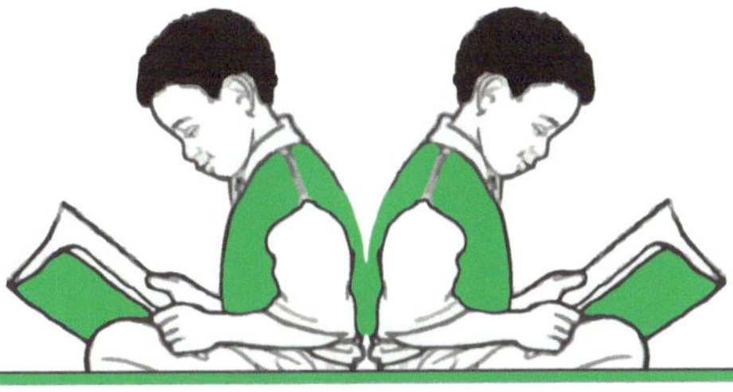

THIS BOOK BELONGS TO

Icon Publishing Limited
P. O. Box OD 972
Odorkor, Accra
Ghana
www.facebook.com/myicongh
www.twitter.com/myicongh
+233 (0)23 3505 055,

iconpublishingltd@gmail.com
iconpublishing@ymail.com
enquiries.icongh@gmail.com

Cover and Interior Design by iCON-gh +233 24 4890 432

ISBN: 978-9988-8566-1-8

ANANSE AND FRIENDS AT THE VILLAGE OF PLENTY

AND ANOTHER TALE FROM AFRICA*

*WHY BEARDS DO NOT GROW ON WOMEN (VERSION 2)

Dan Odei

Kwame Insaidoo

In this Ghanaian folktale Ananse uses tricks to survive the famine in his village.

There was a severe famine all over the land. People were starving for food to eat, and almost everybody was desperately searching for food to eat. But in a small village tucked in the middle of the forest, there was plenty of food, and all the inhabitants in the village had plenty to eat—so much that they threw away the surplus food at night.

Some of the villagers went out of their way to look for other villagers who needed food and found out that Ananse had grown lean and hungry and was dying of hunger. The villagers promised that he would get plenty of food to eat but only on the condition that he would never come to the village by himself but would always bring a friend so they could share in their abundance.

They told him that the villagers did not like selfish people to sneak into their village to eat by themselves; the villagers only helped people who were generous to their friends. The villagers assured Ananse that, if he did not bring a friend when he came to eat, he would be chased out of the village and barred from ever visiting again. The villagers assured Ananse that they had enormous amounts of food in their village, so in order for the villagers to know what kind of food Ananse and his friends liked, they should sing a song that would tell the cooks in the village what food they wanted to eat that day. Ananse thanked the people and bade them farewell, promising that he would be back soon with his best friend.

When Ananse went home he called his best friend, the dog, and reported, "Hey, Dog, we are sitting in this godforsaken town, starving with practically nothing to eat from sunup till sundown. I have found a secret place for us to go and eat all we can eat tomorrow if only you will listen and do exactly what I tell you to do once we get to the secret village."

The dog promised Ananse that he would do whatever he was told to do as long as he could get some food to eat. Ananse began by telling the dog that when they reached the outskirts of the village, he had to sing the following song to the villagers:

I am the big, bad dog from the bush
And all I am trained to eat from birth

Is garbage, rotten bones
And people's day-old meat
And foul, rotten guts of sick animals
I swear to you, provide me with these
And I will demonstrate to you
That I will never stop eating these foods

The dog sang this song over and over as he and Ananse made their way to the village, and he was delighted at the prospect of finally getting some food to eat. He never even bothered to ask Ananse what song he would sing once they got to the village.

They eventually got to the outskirts of the village where all the cooks were ready to hear the songs of Ananse and his best friend so they could begin to prepare their choice of food for them. Ananse prompted the dog to begin his song so the villagers would prepare his food; thereupon the dog began to sing his well-rehearsed song:

I am the big, bad dog from the bush
And all I am trained to eat from birth
Is garbage, rotten bones,

And people's day-old meat
And foul, rotten guts of sick animals.
I swear to you, provide me with these
And I will demonstrate to you
That I will never stop eating these foods.

When he finished singing, Ananse told him to sing loudly again so the sleeping cooks and the chief would hear it and prepare his food for him. The dog sang the song so loudly that people in the village began laughing about his poor choice of food.

When Ananse's turn came, he sang:

I am the same good old Ananse
Who has travelled to your village
Filled with good and kind-hearted people.
All I eat daily is roasted chicken
Fresh eggs, juicy steaks, and baked lamb meat
And, while you are at it, throw in
Some of your best brewed liquor in the village
For Ananse loves you forever

The two reached the chief's house, where their foods were prepared, and the villagers had given all the garbage, rotten bones, and guts from decayed animals to the dog and asked him to eat. Ananse got what he asked for: juicy steak, freshly baked chicken, fresh eggs, and the best brewed liquor in the village. When the dog glanced at Ananse's food, it looked fresh, palatable, and delicious indeed; that was the food he also wished he had, so he asked the villagers why Ananse had gotten a better choice of food.

The villagers answered by telling him, "You got what you asked for because over here we deliver exactly what you ask for. You see, Ananse asked for the best food in the village so we gave him what his heart desired. And you asked only for rotten bones and the guts of decayed animals, so we gave you what you asked for." They advised the dog, "In our village, you have to be careful what you ask for because you will get exactly what you ask for."

The dog begged Ananse for some of his food, which made Ananse angry, so he threw some hot pepper in the dog's eyes and told him to shut up and eat the food he had asked for. The dog was reluctant to eat his food, but the villagers compelled him to eat what

*Ananse eating the best food in the village whiles the dog is served
rotten bones and the guts of decayed animals.*

he asked for; so he forced himself to eat his rotten food, while Ananse consumed his delicious food with ravenous haste. They thanked the villagers and left for their town. When they got back to their town, the dog angrily told the cat how Ananse had cleverly deceived him during the dinner at the village of plenty. He told the cat to be careful of Ananse because he was not really a good friend but a trickster and an imposter.

The next day Ananse called upon the cat and informed him about the secret village filled with all kinds of sumptuous food and invited him to go there for the feast of a lifetime. The cat agreed to accompany Ananse to the village, but he secretly swore to himself that Ananse would never outwit him and that he would be himself and let the villagers know what food he wanted to eat. Ananse began by telling the cat how much he loved him and respected him, adding, "You know I have many friends, but I genuinely love you. That is why I am helping you to get over your hunger by taking you to a special village where there is abundant food for you. I want you to believe what I have to tell you about this village: they have an enormous supply of food and meat, and they love to hear you sing. This is the song I have arranged for you:

I am a cat, and I love my masters
Who keep me inside and care for me
As I come to your village today
I pray for all your leftover food and rotten meat
The rotten meat and food you are discarding

As Ananse was coaching the cat about the song to sing when they arrived at the village, the cat smiled and asked Ananse what he would say to the villagers when he got there. But Ananse told him that he was still thinking about his song and would tell him later during the day. The cat thanked Ananse for his generous help in taking him to the village of plenty and assured him that he would sing the song as instructcd.

At long last, after walking for miles they reached the outskirts of the village of plenty. Ananse asked the Cat to begin his song for the people to begin preparing his food for him. The cat began:

I am an old wise cat with seven lives
I have lived on earth for centuries
But my friends think I am a fool
And want to think for me, but that's their mistake
From the dawn of life, I have gotten only the best
The best food, like fresh milk, fresh chicken
Fresh fish, fresh meat, and all the best food you have
I need some cold ice water too
And God bless all of you
With much love from your beloved cat

When Ananse heard the cat singing his song, he became enraged and screamed, "No, no, no! That is not the song I taught you to sing, you stupid cat! Follow what I taught you and don't deviate from my teachings." But the old, wise cat ignored Ananse and continued loudly to sing his song again and again, making sure that all the villagers heard his request.

Ananse was devastated because he had no choice but to sing the alternate song of eating the residue of the cat's food. Ananse jealously watched as the cat ate his sumptuous food, while he had to make do with rotten bones and discarded food. The cat ate rapidly because

*A devastated Ananse questioning why the cat is singing a
different song*

he was scared of what Ananse might do to him; he used his legs to protect the food but continued to eat all his food hurriedly. The cat's fear of Ananse explains why he always eats rapidly and protects his food with his legs.

The core moral lesson here is that we should never allow our friends—or anyone, for that matter—to define who we are or to tell us what our dreams and goals should be. Instead we should try to think for ourselves. People may advise us, but they cannot and must not be allowed to define who we are. We must learn to think responsibly for ourselves. It is almost a crime for anyone to parrot what others do and say without thinking for themselves. If the dog had learned to think for himself, he would not have been misled by Ananse into asking for rotten bones and the guts of decayed animals, which he did not really want.

It is also important for us to examine the motives of so-called friends who come to us with all kinds of gifts and 'wise' ideas. We must not thoughtlessly follow them and get ourselves into trouble. Instead, we must learn to think for ourselves, and when confronted with wise ideas, we must ask ourselves what they want from us, why they are coming to us, whether they normally come to us with ideas, and what kind of people they are: sincere or deceptive.

You see, Ananse was not really a sincere friend of the dog or the cat; a sincere friend would not tell his friends to ask for rotten food, while he asked for the most delicious food in the village of plenty. A sincere friend would have made sure that he and his friends got only the best food to eat.

Answer the following questions:

1. What was required of Ananse in order to get plenty and consistent food supply?
2. a) Which best friend did Ananse first take along to the village of plenty?
   b) What kind of food was he served and why?
   c) Was he happy about it?
3. a) Did the cat obey Ananse's instructions?
   b) Why or why not?
4. What kind of food did Ananse eat when he visited the village of plenty with the cat?
5. Why does the cat eat rapidly and always protect his food with his legs?
6. What have you learned from this folktale?
7. Find the meaning of the following words in the dictionary and use them in your own sentences;
   i. Desperately
   ii. Inhabitants
   iii. Tyrannical
   iv. Sneak
   v. Godforsaken
   vi. Outskirts
   vii. Rehearsed
   viii. Steaks

ix. Palatable

x. Reluctant

xi. Compelled

xii. Ravenous

xiii. Imposter

xiv. Sumptuous

xv. Enormous

xvi. Enraged

xvii. Deviate

xviii. Devastated

8. Which of the following questions is not answered in the story?

    a) What did the people in the small village do with their surplus food?

    b) What did Ananse do to the cat when the cat refused to follow his instructions?

    c) What assurance did the dog give when Ananse first told him about the village of plenty?

    d) What did the dog do when he realised that he had been deceived by Ananse?

WHY BEARDS DO NOT GROW ON WOMEN
(VERSION TWO)

This Nigerian folktale concerns the importance of honesty.

Many years ago, women grew beards, and some in positions of authority were required to wear beards as a condition of their employment. Indeed the women's beards were so long and curly that they looked more attractive than those of the men. Some of the women even used their beards as their purses. These bearded women lived peacefully with their brethren in a powerful kingdom under the leadership of their beloved, benevolent King Akeem.

The king was so merciful to his subjects that he shared most of his wealth with the poor inhabitants of his kingdom. The symbol of his authority was a small diamond ring shaped like an elephant tusk, which he appropriately named "the tusk," and that he had inherited from his great grandfather. He valued the tusk so much that he stored it in a covered clay dish and ensured that his servants meticulously washed it in the nearby stream on daily basis.

One day King Akeem had an important ceremony to attend, and he rushed to the ceremony without leaving any instructions for his servants regarding the valuable contents of his clay dish. New servants were waiting on him that day, and they did not know that they had to remove the diamond ring before cleaning the dish. In order to please the king, they sped to the stream to hurriedly clean the dish and return it to the palace before the king arrived. Unfortunately, for them, just as they opened the clay dish, the diamond ring fell into the muddy waters. In their desperation to retrieve the ring, they swam all over the muddy stream but could not find the ring, so they went home to report the loss to their king, who became ill at the thought that they had lost his symbol of authority.

The king could not live without this symbol of his authority; so he first offered a handsome reward to anybody in the kingdom who found his ring, and then he organized a large search party of the best fishermen, swimmers, and divers to search for his kingly tusk. The search party spent two solid months looking for the ring but could not find it, which made the king so powerless that a nearby enemy pounced on his people in a tribal war and defeated his kingdom. He was taken a captive but was released after his elders paid a hefty ransom to the victorious tribe.

Even though he remained king, his powers gradually waned because the elders were secretly contriving to depose him unless he was able to retrieve his lost symbol of power.

One sunny day, a little girl went fishing and was overjoyed to catch a large fish, but much to her surprise, the fish spoke to her.

"You, nice little girl," the fish said, "Are not going to kill me, because if you spare my life, I will give you a handsome prize that will make you rich and famous." The fear that gripped the little girl made her drop the fish back into the muddy stream, and true to its word, the fish went down into the water, brought back the king's diamond ring, and gave it to the frightened little girl. The little girl took the ring and began running home to her parents to give it to them, but on her way home she met a bearded woman, who forcefully took the ring from her hand and warned her not to mention it to anybody, because the day she did, she would surely die. The woman hid the precious ring in her beard and went on her way.

A fish speaking to the girl from inside the net

When the little girl got home, she told her father what had happened to her in the stream, all about the fish and the ring and how a bearded woman had seized the ring from her. Her father immediately went to King Akeem to relate what his daughter had told him. The king was overjoyed, and he and all his elders went to the bearded woman's house to ask for the ring. The woman told them that she did not have a ring. She claimed that the little girl was lying and that she had not seen the girl for the past week, but the girl insisted that she had taken the ring from her.

The elders searched the whole house and found no ring, so they decided to leave the woman alone, believing her story and thinking that the little girl must just have been hallucinating or trying to get the king's attention. But just as they were about to leave, the girl's father suggested that the elders search the woman's unkempt beard. A thorough search of her beard revealed that the king's diamond ring, his beloved elephant tusk, was indeed hidden in her beard.

The king's elders decided to punish the woman for concealing the king's precious ring, but King Akeem pardoned her. Instead he decreed that no woman would be allowed to wear a beard, and he ordered all women to shave their beards and treat their faces with special herbs from the forest to prevent their beards from growing. From that day onward, women could not grow beards anymore, and King Akeem became powerful and famous once again.

Moral Lessons

The moral here is simply that honesty is the best policy. If the bearded woman had been honest, she would not have taken the ring from the little girl and then warned her not to talk to her parents about it. She would have escorted the girl to their benevolent king, who could have rewarded all of them, and the woman could have then become a trusted and an important member of the kingdom. She could have made a good name for herself. As our elders say, a good name is better than riches.

Answer the following questions:

1. To what use did some of the women who lived in King Akeem's era put their beard?

2. a) What was the symbol of authority for King Akeem?

   b) What name did he assign to it?

3. a) Describe how the king's symbol of authority ended up in the stream?

   b) Did the king's search party yield any desired result?

4. Even though Akeem remained king, what was happening to his authority?

5. Why was the little girl afraid of the big fish it had caught?

6. What obstacle did the little girl encounter as she run home with her gift?

7. How did King Akeem react upon hearing that his symbol of authority has been found?

8. a) What lies did the woman tell King Akeem and
    his elders?

    b) Where and how was the ring found in the
    woman's house?

    c) What punishment was given to her?

9. What have you learned from this folktale?

10. Find the meaning of the following words in the
    dictionary and use them in sentences of your
    own,

    i. Tusk

    ii. Meticulously

    iii. Hefty

    iv. Waned

    v. Hallucinating

11. The main purpose of paragraph one is to

    a. show how important King Akeem was

    b. describe how the king lost his diamond ring

    c. give some information on a phenomenon
    that no longer exists

    d. show how a particular woman found the
    king's ring.

12. Provide words that could have been used in place of the following words in the story,

    a. attractive — (paragraph one)

    b. benevolent — (paragraph one)

    c. wealth — (paragraph two)

    d. hurriedly — (paragraph three)

    e. waned — (paragraph five)

    f. overjoyed — (paragraph six)

    g. concealing — (paragraph ten)

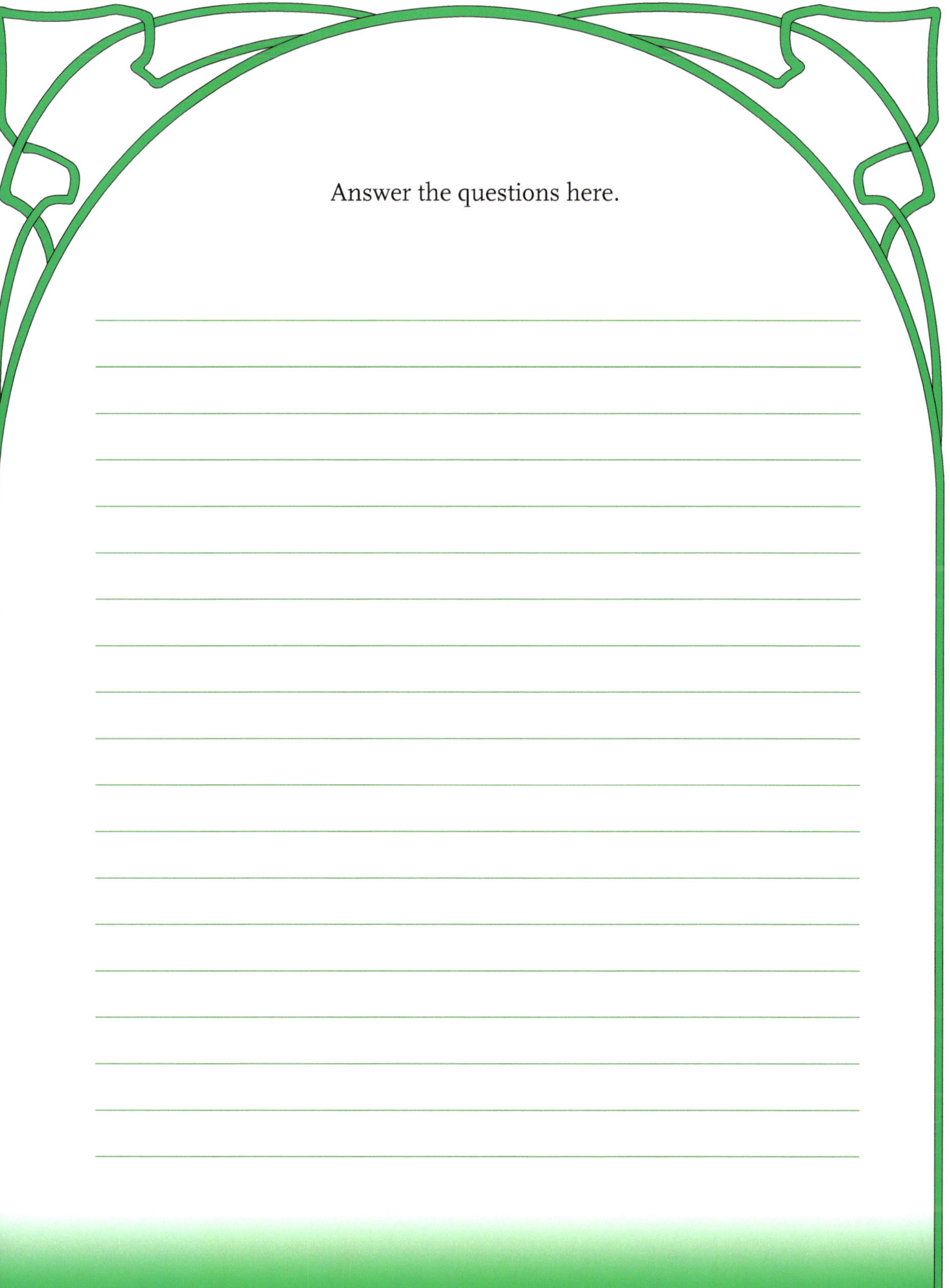

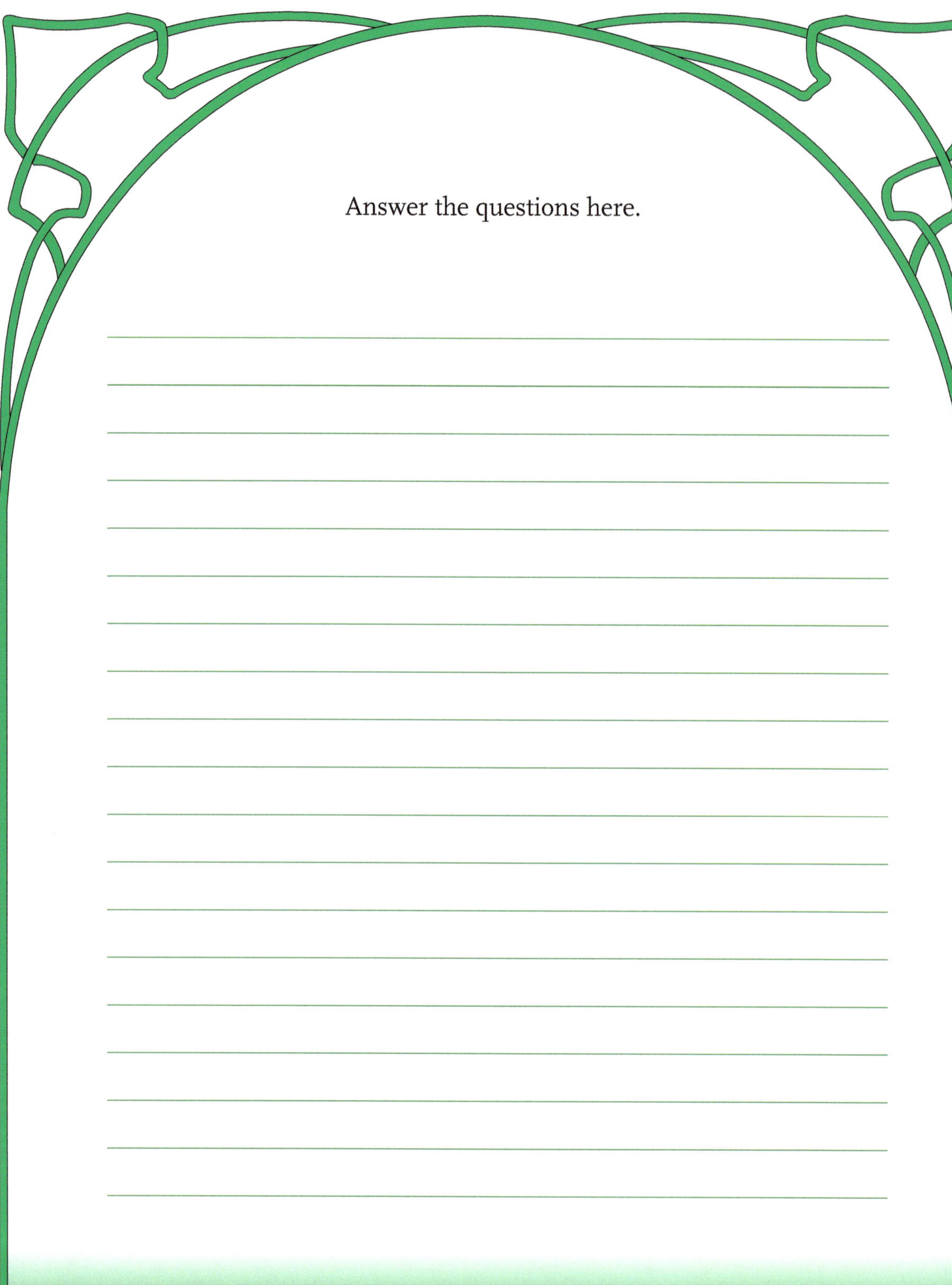

Answer the questions here.